# ONCE UPON IN OUR MINDS

Authors

Saanchi Singh | Namit Jagirdar | Aabha Ghuli | Anshika Iyer

Aadhya Garg | Shiza Fatima | Shreelekha Shinde | Jinal Shah



RIDHZWORLD
PUBLISHING

First published in 2023 by
RidhzWorld Publishing
Hadapsar, Pune, India
www.ridhzworld.com



ISBN: 987-81-962000-3-9

# ACKNOWLEDGEMENT

Ridhzworld Publishing takes pride in bringing forward the stories of our new-age authors and hoping this opportunity encourages more and more children to be creative and engage in meaningful expressions of their thoughts.

In today's modern world, where innovation and creativity are at an all-time high, there are emerging trends associated with fostering great minds from an early age. Such aspiring minds can now grow, expand, and create creatives works, independent of their age. One such collection is this newly released anthology book - an amazing compilation of short stories written by talented young writers, all scintillating in their own individual ways.

"Once Upon In Our Minds' story writing competition, was an initiative at age of 8 years by Author Ridhhaan Jaiin, Founder of RidhzWorld publishing with supporting partners Kubic Online Edutech, Make Way Marketing, Nanhaa Gyan Foundation, schools, and social media influencers.

The competition was held to encourage motivated and enthusiastic children, aged between 5 to 12 recall their imaginary adventures and weave them into palatable stories.

This competition has functioned as a platform for the students to express themselves in a unique and spectacular manner. The stories found in this anthology are indeed thrilling, funny, and full of emotion. Thanks to our esteem judges Divya Nair, Priyanka Joshi, and Ankita Manna for shortlisting these incredible stories.

Readers can be sure to indulge in mind-stirring tales of imagination and awe! As the upcoming generation of authors take their place in the world and create revolutionary works, this anthology will be one of many steppingstones!

At RidhzWorld Publishing, we are passionate about book publishing, audiobook creation, marketing, and mass media. Our mission is to empower minds to reach audiences through books, audiobooks, or visual media.

We believe that books, and the stories and ideas they hold, have the unique capacity to connect us, change us, and carry us toward a better future for generations to come. That is why we are committed to working with authors and publishers from all over the world to create books that will resonate with readers everywhere. We want you to follow your passion and
eave rest on us.

---

***Radhicka V Jain***
***Co-Founder, RidhzWorld Publishing***

# FOREWORD

It is my utmost pleasure to introduce the incredible and inspiring work of my budding young writers. Their enthusiasm to express their creativity is evident in the diverse collection of stories in this anthology.
I'm absolutely delighted to have pulled off this year's edition of the "Once Upon In Our Minds" story writing competition with great success! Every participating writer from all over the world put forward some incredible stories that impressively showcased their vivid imaginations and creative flair.

While reading this book I was spellbound by such captivating adventures, every story had a unique and beautiful message from horror to comedy, friendship to mystery, and a variety of other genres. Each coming complete with life-lessons and happy endings that made me smile each time.
I am glad that this book will enable these stories to be shared with a wider audience and inspire others to use the power of writing to convey their messages.

An immense thank you goes out to all my partners, judges, schools, influencers and especially my parents for trusting in my vision and making it come true. Huge congratulations to our winners and all other participants who courageously shared their stories with us during this competition season! Here's a round of applause for everyone involved with "Once Upon In Our Minds!"

***AU Ridhhaan Jaiin***
***Founder, RidhzWorld Publishing***

# Table Of Content


1 **Fruits of the Junk Deed**
Namit Jagirdar | Pg 1

2 **The Sunken Hope**
Aabha Ghuli | Pg 5

3 **The Mighty Gods**
Saanchi Singh | Pg 9

4 **The King of Thefts**
Aadhya Garg | Pg 13

5 **Adventures of Ammu**
Anshika Iyer | Pg 23

6 **Metamorphosis**
Shreelekha Shinde | Pg 31

7 **Saviours of the World**
Jinal Shah | Pg 36

8 **One Small Action**
Shiza Fatima | Pg 48

# Fruits of the Junk Deed

By

Namit Jagirdar

On a late evening, two best friends Rahul and Neyan were returning from their football coaching. Both, were very tired and hungry too. While walking they took a quick snack break which would give them some instant energy. They sat on a bench and opened their bags. Neyan took out a packet of chips along with some biscuits, while Rahul had a banana and an apple. They finished their snacks and started walking again towards their home.

This was the routine followed for next 4 days. Then later that evening, when Rahul reached home, he told his mom, "Mom, I don't wish to have those apples and bananas, or any other fruit, please buy me some flavourful chips". To this his mom responded, "Rahul you are at a growing age and as you are playing sports you need a good diet so that you have a great stamina to play and keep your body energetic. Junk food like chips, biscuits do not give you enough energy and makes your body a garbage of junk food." Rahul was very upset and did not agree on the same and went back to his room and started working on his project.

On the next day, after returning from the school, Rahul's mom gave him Rs. 100 and asked him to get his favourite fruit. Rahul obediently left for the market and headed towards a departmental store, there he used the money on buying packets of chips and biscuits which he wanted to have. Later he sat outside the departmental store and finished all the things that he bought. When he reached home, his mother asked, "Which fruits did you buy Rahul?". Rahul looked worried, he answered, "Mom, by the time I reached the market, I found out that I had misplaced the money that you gave me, it fell from my pocket and I did not realize the same. I searched for it but all in vain". His mother consoled him and said, "Don't worry my son it happens and ensure that you learn a lesson from this and take care so that the same thing is not repeated."

Almost after a week, Mom again gave Rahul some money and asked him to get some fruits of his choice from the market. Again, as Rahul got a chance, he did the same thing and returned home saying he lost the money. His Mom doubted and she understood there is something that he's hiding from her. She thought to talk to him calmly and asked him what happened exactly. So that day post dinner, Mom went to Rahul's room and asked him, "Rahul, there is something that you are hiding from me. You are a responsible boy and I know you won't repeat the same thing again." Listening to these words of his mom Rahul felt guilty and told her the truth. He told her that he had bought junk food from the money he was given for fruits. Later Mom said, "Don't worry my son, I am very proud of you that at least you told me the truth." "Whatever I do, it is for your betterment and there is nothing that I am going to do wrong with you my child". Rahul realized that he did a wrong thing by telling lies to his mother and apologized to her for the same.

## Moral Of The Story

We should always listen to our elders as they care for us and we should not speak lies to them.

# The Sunken Hope

By

Aabha Ghuli

In 1750, there was a boy named John. He was born in India. He moved to England along with his family when he was three. His parents used to tell him fascinating stories about India. His greatest dream was to come back to India. However, there was one big problem, he had to travel to buy a ship called Misafera and it had to cross Somalia. There were many pirates in Somalia. Air transport was not invented yet, so land and water transport were the only options. When John turned twenty-five years, he married a young woman. Her name was Myra. She was born to Indian parents.

When she was twelve years old, she and her parents had gone on an outing. Her father Anthony was the captain of a ship. As Myra and her family passed Somalia, they were attacked by pirates. One of the sea men helped Myra escape but nobody knew about her parents. Myra remembered a pirate. His hair was black and brown with spikes, standing straight like aloe vera. He had a black patch covering one of his eyes and a broken gun just to threaten people. Knowing that the gun could not hurt anyone, Myra teased the pirate. When the pirate fired the gun, only air flew out! This event made Myra laugh till date.

John got a job as a ship architect. After many years, in 1780, Myra gave birth to a beautiful girl. The baby was named Nadia. Nadia didn't have her maternal grandparents, as her mother thought that she had lost her parents forever. Both John and Myra wanted to come back to India to visit their birth places. Myra recollected that every time she was on the ship, her hope for coming to India increased. One day Myra and John planned to come back to India. They tried to find other options, than passing Somalia. But they could not find any. They decided to go by Misafera.

They boarded Misafera at lunch time. When they were checking in, Myra noticed a portrait. She paid no attention to it. Later when she was walking in the lobby with her family, she noticed that there was the same portrait. Myra said, "Hey! John look at that portrait, she looks like my mother". She wondered why it was there. "We will ask about it to the manager during lunch time", John said.

After lunch, while walking back to their room, they met the manager. "Hello", Myra said. "Oh hi! Nice to meet you", the manager replied. "Why is that portrait of my mother over here?" Myra asked. "Mam, they are the ones who designed this ship, they started this", the manager replied. Myra asked, "Where are they?". "In room number 203",
said the manager.

Myra, John and Nadia walked to room number 203, Myra was nervous and excited she knocked on the door. It was her mother who opened the door. Without any doubt her mother recognized Myra. "My dear M...My...Myra" she cried "Yes mother", Myra said. Tears flowing down their eyes, they hugged each other. Myra introduced John and Nadia to her mother. Myra asked her mother how they had survived. Her mother told her that, pirates did not come to attack them, but they were running away from the police.

Everybody reached India happy and safe. John met his parents. Sometimes Myra, her parents, John and Nadia would come for a trip on the ship.

# The Mighty Gods

By

Saanchi Singh

Once upon a time in the ancient ages there used to be two Ganas groups, one was Rakshas and other was Devtas. Rakshas were like we have Mahishasur in the cartoon series Little Singham and Devtas like Ganesha and Krishna. Both Rakshas and Devtas did not like each other and kept fighting over who has more strength. They both fought and Devtas started winning because Krishna used to have a lot of milk and butter, which made him strong. Similarly, Lord Ganesha used to have laddoos like the cartoon character Chhota Bheem so he was also very powerful.

Later as the fight progressed one guru named Shukracharya came and helped the Rakshas. With the help of Guru Shukracharya, Rakshas started winning. Devtas were sad and went to Lord Vishnu for help. Lord Vishnu suggested the Devtas to start Samudra Manthan. Lord Vishu told them that many gifts like Skate Boards, Pencil Boxes, Chocolates will come out of Samudra Manthan and Amrit will also be one of the gifts. Amrit is a magical drink which is more powerful than milk. Amrit will only be given to Devtas as the Amrit Kalash pot has a scanner to identify who is a Rakshas and who is a Devta. Devtas will have Amrit and will never get defeated.

Two Rakshas named Raahu and Ketu wanted to have Amrit but the kalash scanned them and found that they are Rakshas, so scolded them and told them to go away at once. They felt very sad but got an idea that they should go to a beauty parlour. Both of them went to a beauty parlour, put some deo and got dressed nicely so that they looked like Devtas. Amrit kalash scanned them and could not identify them as Rakshas and both Raahu and Ketu drank Amrit. As soon as Raahu and Ketu drank Amrit they started dancing and became their original self.

All Devtas got worried and went to Lord Mahadev for help. Mahadev advised Rahu and Ketu that they should not cheat. Cheating is a very bad habit, it will help you in the short run however, will fail you in the long run of life. Now that they had the Amrit, he could only make the effect less. Mahadev told the devtas since Sun and Moon are rising and setting every day that means they enjoy travelling a lot. And do not enjoy studies. This way Raahu and Ketu can only create problems for Sun and Moon. All other Devtas will not get into any kind of problem.

Since that time Raahu and Ketu come and go to create problems in form of eclipse for the Sun and Moon. As Raahu and Ketu are Rakshas, we have to clean our house and take bath after eclipse is over.

# The King of Thefts

By

Aadhya Garg

# Chapter 1

The summer holidays had just started, and Jenny was playing chess with her friend, Sarah, who stayed in the same apartment, when her phone rang.

She picked it up, while moving her Queen, to checkmate the Black King. “Hello,” Jenny said. “Hello, it’s me, Lisa.
Are you alone?” Asked Lisa, in a very tense voice. “Nope,” said Jenny, “I’m playing chess. Is it that important?” Jenny asked, getting up.

“Yes!” said Lisa. It was time for Sarah to go home. Jenny asked Lisa what the matter was.

“You know the famous Mona Lisa painting that was part of the special exhibit in the museum?
Well, guess what? It was stolen from the museum sometime back. My aunt was there when the news broke!” Lisa said breathlessly.

“O. M. G!” exclaimed Jenny. “You better come here then. It’ll hardly take you a minute.” Lisa came. Just then, Jenny got another phone call.

# Chapter 2

“Hello, Mr. Jones!” called the voice. “Excuse me?” replied Jenny.

“Is this Inspector Jones speaking?” The American voice came again. Jenny was surprised, guessing who would be calling the Inspector at such an odd time, and was very curious to know what the man wanted to say.

Who knows, they might solve this mystery too! Luckily, she had seen and heard Mr. Jones’ voice on television so she knew how it sounded. She imitated him. “Oh yes!” she said. “What happened?” “Sir, the famous Mona Lisa painting got stolen today, and we have found footprints! Size ten ones! And, we’ve scanned a handprint as well! I’ll message the image to you.”

The agent replied urgently. “Oh, I see,” said Jenny, still imitating. “I’m a bit busy right now, so I’ll call you later.” She saved the image on to her phone, and deleted the contact number, so they couldn’t track her down. Jenny told Lisa all that had happened.

Meanwhile, the agent went to the police station, and asked the real Mr. Jones, what he thought about his findings.

“What on earth are you talking about?” He spoke. “I guess you called someone else! We’ve been cheated!”

## Chapter 3

The next day, Jenny and Lisa went to inspect the museum from where the picture was stolen. They found a little notebook on the pearly white floor, under the curtain.

Inside it, a hurried cursive note read -
Jim will give you the millilitre. At exactly half past five. From: Your boss Charlie. They knew that the symbol of millilitre was ml, and ml meant Mona Lisa! They further decoded that a man called Jim would give the thief the painting and their gang leader was called Charlie. They took a photograph of the note and left it where it was and then kept quiet about it. The next day, Jenny was at a sleepover at Lisa's house. Suddenly, the bell rang. Lisa looked through the peephole.
She was horrified. Mr. Jones was standing there, waiting for the door to open. Apparently, he had traced the call to Jenny and tracked her down. Lisa ran to her room and told Jenny the news. Lisa and Jenny hid in the bathroom and latched the door. Lisa's mother opened the door only to see a cop marching into her house in the middle of the night! "We are going to check your house." said Mr. Jones sternly. He checked Lisa's room. It was tidy, and clean, but no one was there. He knocked on the bathroom door. Lisa replied in quite a hoarse voice of an old man, "Who is it? I'm in!" The inspector finally gave up when he got another call from his team. "I am very sorry to disturb you for no reason, but is there an old man in the house?" Mr. Jones asked Lisa's mother. Luckily, Lisa's grandfather had come to visit, so Lisa's mother said yes. Mr. Jones thought that this was the wrong house so he didn't find it worthwhile to ask about any girls.

After making sure the coast was clear, Jenny and Lisa finally came out of their hiding places. They were so relieved that they had escaped.

# Chapter 4

After Jenny left, Lisa was searching on her laptop for more information about the museum. She quickly drew a rough copy of the foot marks Jenny had emailed her, and searched for the brand that made those shoes.

The results were 'Land's End', and 'Matchamisu.' She couldn't decide between the two, and called for a meeting in their secret tent, in Lisa's backyard. Jenny arrived, and after she was told what Lisa found, she suggested they go to the shops, and enquire about who bought their shoes recently. Lisa agreed. They both asked their parents to visit the shops with them, just to see all the things displayed.

Jenny went to Land's End, while Lisa went to Matchamisu. Jenny enquired and found out that a fair, rather short young woman, had come to get them for her brother. Unfortunately, those were size eight! Jenny's family knew the store owner, so he did not object when she asked him for all the people who had bought such shoes from his store.

Only one other person had bought them. Jenny noted the name down and took a picture of the signature on their customer records. A Johnathan Grafton had bought a pair of size ten shoes! He had touched another pair of shoes as well, and Jenny used her DFS (Detective Fingerprint Scanner) app that she and Lisa created. The prints matched the one she had in her photo gallery!!

Now, Jenny got thinking... "I guess the thief wouldn't be a fool, to write his real name, but if he had put a fake signature, he would be caught. And, the signature does look a bit, like 'James G.'"

Meanwhile, Lisa got the result as Frank Wilson. He too, had the same fingerprint! Now, their app could never go wrong, so Lisa was sure he was the culprit.

They both met at a campsite in the forest behind a giant oak tree. They had two small purple separate tents and one spacious orange one

The orange one was for emergencies. They met there of course, and told each other their clues. In the end, both were puzzled.

Then suddenly, Jenny figured it out. "What if Jonathan Grafton and Frank Wilson are the same person in disguise?!" She asked Lisa. Lisa agreed.

And this Frank Wilson's signature looked like James G too! Jenny asked Lisa if James G's 'G' had a big loop, and yes! It did!

# Chapter 5

Jenny suddenly exclaimed, "I could kick myself for not thinking of this before!" "What?" said Lisa.

"What exactly do you mean!?" "Well, let's go through the telephone book in the post office, and find the names there, plus, there must be something related to both the names, and we don't need to see Johnathan Grafton because we know that they are the same person!" "Hmmm," said Lisa. "Okay, I'm not sure if it is relevant, but let's give it a shot. Anyway, see you later, or I'll be late for dinner."

So, the very next day at half past eight in the morning, the two met at the post office, and started searching. "Fannie Uteger, Ferdinand Underwood, Frederick, Freddie, Fred, Fredericia, Frank, Frank, Frank, Frankie, FRANK! My goodness! So many people named Frank!" said Lisa, forgetting to read the surnames.

"There are two Frank Wilsons," said Jenny. "The other two are Simpson and Brown." "Yes," agreed Lisa. "You go to the one at 904, Stanley Apartments, Marylin Street, and I'll go to the one at Hillmore Mansion. At five-thirty SHARP!"

So, at half past five in the evening, Jenny got her cycle out of the basement and rode off to the address. She got a good idea to dress up as a cleaning lady and entered inside.

She rang the bell and a rather shaggy looking man opened the door. "Why didn't that other lady come today?" He asked.

Jenny replied in her fine imitation of Scottish accent, "Sir, she ain't well!"

The man asked her to come inside and get on with the dishes. The time there was actually pretty normal, and Frank showed no sign of suspicious activity at all! Jenny wasn't that sure though, and left her special handmade tracker, that was waterproof, fireproof, and which could even record videos, in one of his shoelaces.

Lisa on the other hand, had dressed as a window cleaner. She had somehow googled up something about him booking a window cleaner for his windows, from Limelight Shine Cleaners, and managed to call the company to not send a cleaner over because he had cancelled the booking! She also found another piece of news. This man was rich and famous!! So why would he have to steal the Mona Lisa?
She definitely thought it might be the other man!

She went dressed as a cleaner and cleaned pretty well! This was the first time she was glad her parents made her do this every day! She was paid a good sum and rejoiced inwardly, but she got over it quickly, and put the duplicate tracker that Jenny had invented, in his shoelace too! While she was at work, she noticed that the man she worked for, was quite rude! "You! Get on with your work fast! I have a meeting to attend, while you here are scrubbing the windows and making noise!!" he shouted. He was also quite suspicious. He suddenly used to get calls, for which he used to run into a room, to pick. Lisa decided to activate her tracker and recorded an audio of what was happening in the room.

She could only catch words like painting, sell, money, thefts, Jim, I will get away, and things like that. But that was more than enough! She was going to call Jenny! And maybe the police soon!

## Chapter 6

After exchanging their notes from both places, they were ready to make an arrest!!

"Rrrrring!!!!" The phone rang at the police station. Inspector Arthur Jones picked up.

"Hello!" He said. "What's the emergency?" Jenny smiled and said, "There isn't any emergency, but we solved the Mystery of the Missing Picture! About the Mona Lisa!"

The inspector listened to the details and the two of them were suitably rewarded!
This was certainly a good vacation!

They had managed to solve the king of all thefts!

# Adventures of Ammu

By

Anshika Iyer

## Chapter 1: The Campus

"How much longer?" cried Ammu holding her waist and panting. "My feet are hurting and I cannot walk anymore" "Just a little more" said her mother, "See, we have almost reached...!" pointing at a tower in a distance. "You see that tower, right? That's where we are headed. Now put your best foot forward and let's get moving", said her father. Ammu was a sharp and intelligent nine-year-old. She had a thing for puzzles and was extremely curious. She loved reading books of mystery and intrigue. She and her parents were visiting her maternal grandparents in Pune who lived right next to the sprawling Pune University campus.

This morning, Ammu's father thought it would be a good idea to take a morning walk inside the University campus. "Wow, this place is huge", cried Ammu, her eyes wide... And so green" "Yes, Ammu, this place used to be the headquarters of the British Government in Pune in the pre-independence era", said mother, "It has five gates and if one doesn't know the way, it is so easy to get lost...! So, keep up now...!" "Ok ma", said Ammu, striding briskly attempting to keep up with her parents...! She had no intention of getting lost in this huge place...! Her father chuckled looking at her worried expression, "We are not in a forest, Ammu. This is a campus. People come here to study and work by the hundreds every day, don't worry, you won't get lost, but hurry, we have to reach the main building. I do want to look around a little bit." Ammu was amazed at the size of the campus. The pathway was huge and was dotted with trees and lots of greenery. As she walked along the pathway, Ammu could hear the chirping of birds and squirrels. After a while Ammu and her parents reached the main building which looked like an old heritage structure made out of stone.

The building also had a huge and tall tower with the Indian flag fluttering in the wind.

Extremely excited and inquisitive that she was, Ammu looked forward to seeing the building from the inside. She walked up to the building; however, she was disappointed to see the doors and the windows bolted shut. "Can we not see the building from the inside? she asked.

"No Ammu, we cannot", said her father.
This is a working campus and at 7 in the morning, it is bound to remain shut. Let us look around a little bit and then head back. I'm famished and can do with a big breakfast."

Ammu peeked into one of the windows and saw a table with some books on it. One of the books had a strange yellow glow coming out of it. She dismissed it thinking it was a trick of the light, however, her curious mind made her wonder whether those books actually belonged to the British, when they used this building as their office.

She decided that she must somehow get into the room and take a look at the books.

She tried to turn the knob of one of the doors, to open it and enter the room but it was locked. A dejected Ammu ran back to her parents, who were taking a walk in the garden outside the building.

## Chapter 2: The Curious Mind

"Ma, I saw some books on the table in the University building. What could they be about. Can we come back again tomorrow to, see?" "No Ammu", her mother said laughing.

"Your father has already explained that this is a working campus. People study and work here. I can see that brain of yours is already working overtime". While back home with her parents, Ammu couldn't stop thinking about the room and the books all along. She was certain those books were special and couldn't wait to read them. That night, she kept tossing and turning, her mind still stuck at the University room and the books on the table.

"Oh Ammu, don't fidget so much. Go to sleep", said her grandmother. "Amma, I have to see the books, I can't stop thinking about it." cried Ammu. "Well, go back tomorrow", grunted her grandmother impatiently, "but sleep now".

She tried settling down, but she could not think of anything else. Her mind was too excited as she imagined the book having stories about the kings and queens that ruled England. Or did it have stories and pictures about the kingdoms in India and who they were ruled by?

"No, I just got to know", thought Ammu leaping out of bed quietly careful not to make a sound. After making sure that the household was fast asleep, Ammu pulled out her pink jacket, her shoes and picked up a flashlight determined to make her way to the University. She just had to read those books.

## Chapter 3: Midnight Adventure

Determined to the core, Ammu went alone that night with the flashlight, to the building in the University. "Why is there nobody around?" she thought seeing the gate unmanned and with no security outside.

She remembered her mother's warning that morning, that it was so easy to get lost in the vast space. This scared her a bit, but she ventured on determined to keep to the known track. She wished she had carried some chalk to mark the path she was taking. Teeth chattering slightly, feeling anxious but excited she made her way to the main building. "Strange", thought Ammu, there is nobody at the main building either.

She had an overwhelming sense of being alone, still being watched. She did not like the feeling one bit and momentarily regretted her impulsive decision to visit the University that night. "But I'm here", she sighed, "Might as well explore and check out the mysterious room with the book", making her way quietly through the corridor leading to the room.

She slowly turned the knob to open without making any noise and raising any alarm. It was open. "What! but it was locked in the morning." she thought. "Something strange is definitely going on". Her common sense told her to rush back home, but she was drawn to a heap of books lying on the table like a moth to a flame. The book glowed a bright amber and she gazed at it transfixed. The effect was almost hypnotic. Out of extreme curiosity, Ammu opened the big, old book and turned a couple of pages to look for pictures. Suddenly, she saw a big bright glow coming out of the book. She shielded her eyes against the bright light, but it had blinded her temporarily. Ammu felt like she was getting sucked into the book and let out a loud scream, "Aaaarghhhhh, someone help!"

# Chapter 4: 1930

Ammu could hear shouts of “Vande Mataram”. It rang in chorus as she opened her eyes. To her amazement, she found herself sitting among a group of people with Mahatma Gandhi who was addressing the group. She pinched herself not sure if it was a dream, “Ouch! that hurt!”, she thought. Gandhiji spoke and encouraged each person present to join him in a non-violent protest march against the salt tax levied by the British. His face was so calm and serene and what a soft voice, still a personality magnetic enough to capture the attention and influence such a large crowd! “But where am I? And what am I doing here? “, she wondered Not wanting to be embarrassed in front of the group, Ammu quietly asked the person sitting next to her “What day is it today and where are we?” He looked surprised and told her in a rather angry tone “Today is 12th March 1930 and we are at the Sabarmati Ashram. Gandhiji is giving a call to join the Civil Disobedience Movement against the British.” Ammu joined Gandhiji and thousands of people, as they walked from Sabarmati Ashram to Dandi in Gujarat. On April 6, 1930, at Dandi, Gandhiji made salt by evaporating the sea water, thereby defying the salt tax. Ammu joined Gandhiji as he walked further to the Dharasana Salt Works, a little farther away from Dandi.

On the night of 4th May 1930, the British arrested Gandhiji and the group which accompanied him, before they reached the Dharasana Salt Works. Ammu was also among those who were arrested. Strangely, she did not feel scared or anxious. She felt proud of being able to serve the country. While in jail, Ammu shouted slogans of ‘Vande Mataram’ and ‘Jai Hind’ along with the group. She eventually fell asleep while the group continued the chanting and singing patriotic songs. After a while, she woke up feeling thirsty. She looked around hoping to find Gandhiji and the group also resting.

## Chapter 5: A Surprising turn of events

To her surprise, Ammu found herself on the bed in her grandmother's bedroom. "Where is everyone? I can hear them, but why can I not see them?" she wondered as she heard slogans of 'Vande Mataram' and 'Jai Hind' echoing throughout the house.

Ammu jumped out of the bed and ran to the hall to find her grandparents and parents watching the Prime Minister hoist the national flag and speak to every Indian citizen on the occasion of Azadi Ka Amrit Mahotsav i.e., the 75th year of Indian Independence.

It was August 15th, 2022. "What is going on?", she wondered. "Was that all a dream?" "Ammu, what happened?", asked her grandfather. "You look like you have seen a ghost!"

Ammu gulped and with a shaky voice narrated the confusing and surprising events of the previous night.

They all had a hearty laugh. "Why Ammu, it was all a dream!", said her grandmother. "You were muttering in your sleep though. You and your overactive imagination!". "You got lucky", her grandfather said. "You got to participate in the Salt Satyagraha of 1930, that's when I was a little boy and India got her independence in August 1947."

Everyone laughed loudly as the family moved to the dining room to have their breakfast.

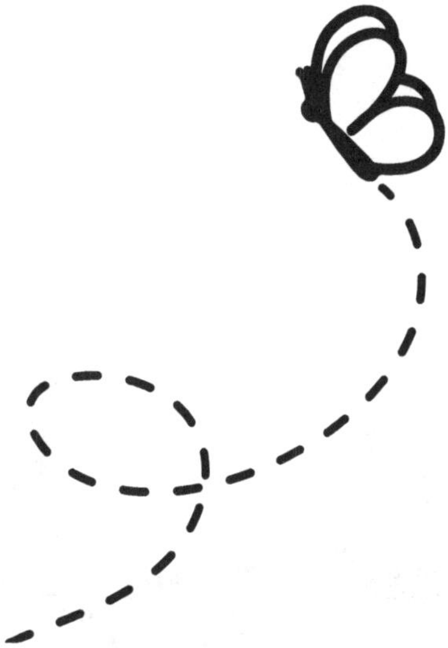

# Metamorphosis

By

Shreelekha Shinde

My mother died just a few days after I was born. They told me that she was perfect, that she was so beautiful that everyone followed her, trying to catch her as if she was a grand prize. They said that she charmed everyone who saw her and was as spirited and colourful as the flowers she adored. I believed I was the complete opposite. My life started under the shade of nature.

Back then, I was just a little egg with no ambitions or talents. I simply existed. When they came, they laughed and smiled, making fun of my helplessness, my tininess. I was just a little blotch on a leaf, they said. Nothing more, nothing less. As the days passed by, I thought of their words, wishing I was something more, something like them, something that was whole and pretty like my mother. I wanted her to be proud of me. It was as if I could see her frowning at me from the great blue sky. It was then that I decided that I had to get out. I stretched myself out and pushed the dense cyst that had formed around me. I remember thinking to myself that it was now or never. I contorted my feeble body into different shapes and sizes till I was completely worn out. These contortions I believe were what caused my then inexplainable hunger. I was draining the life out of myself but I didn't stop. I couldn't stop. My mind gave birth to my goal while my body strained to achieve it. I grew in size steadily and suddenly popped out of my egg. It was like my life had been fulfilled. Not only was I happy but I was sure I had made my mother proud.

That was until, I looked over at them. They too had grown during my self-inflicted exile. They had turned into something far more advanced with wings and antennae with smooth, supple and bejewelled bodies. They had grown mature and wise too. They didn't bother me anymore. They never even glanced at me, at what I had become.

My thirst to prove myself slowly diminished. I felt useless. I felt like a disease that everyone would try to avoid. I tried not to believe my life was meaningless.

But it was. Just as meaningless as it was to compare myself to those other creatures. I wouldn't be able to say that I looked up to them but, I think a small part of me wished that maybe someday I would be able to match their grandeur. As these thoughts enveloped me, I couldn't help but notice how different things were. The leaves which I so lovingly called scrawny. The sky above my head seemed just a wee bit unimpressive.

I was growing haughty and proud and before I knew, I had turned into them. I had turned into a bully, an oppressor, a hurt yet mean splotch, and I never even realized it. Looking back on it now, I think I could've handled the disappointment in a better way but as many people say "The abused, become the abuser and the tormented become the tormentor."

Again, I saw things changing around me. It felt as if the whole world was revolving around me but I was stationary. Right, where I had left myself to my own devices in fatigue and failed potential. I knew I had to do something to get myself out of that endless cycle, but I didn't know how to. Sooner or later, I became numb. I couldn't feel, think or at that point even see or smell anything. I wound all my emotions up into a tiny ball and tucked them away into my heart.

I withdrew from my surroundings and bottled myself up into a soft shell which was dark and strange. Back then, I didn't know what it was called but, it was a chrysalis, MY chrysalis.

Again, I believe I was a little short on thoughts and memory then, so I estimated that I was in the chrysalis for many moons. It was kind of my home away from home and I'm not sure how I felt about it. To this day, I wouldn't be able to describe to you how it felt to be in there. It was a feeling like no other, a kind of exhilaration and fear and excitement all packed into a box and suddenly one day I burst out. My whole body was trembling as I emerged from my confinement and yes the part you all have been waiting for, I spread my new and amazing majestic wings into the air and exhaled a sigh of relief.

My wings were perfect. A beautiful cerulean blue, just like the Pacific Ocean. Like Poseidon himself had bestowed upon me that lovely hue. It was then that I realized how beautiful my mother had been. As I slowly observed my improved body, I felt pure joy and no resentment at all. I had forgotten about my past. It was as if a new creature had emerged from the chrysalis. A blank slate. And as I navigated the skies, I could only ever think of how finally everything had fallen in to place and now, as I write my life's story, I can barely wait to see what happens next.

# Saviours of the World

By

Jinal Shah

# Introduction

Years ago, the Earth was dominated, tortured, and attacked by nasty monsters and villains from different alien & dwarf planets but how will it be written and told to people if there are no heroes. The superheroes of the earth were "The Quadruplets Squadron."

It consisted of the powers of dream catching, being a perfectionist, being able to control a big spirit, read other people's brains, and many more... Their sworn enemy was the Queen of Darkness of the Plutonian mountains of Pluto whose name was Agrona.

The Quadruplets Squadron had defeated her once but after losing, Agrona swore to take a revenge. After many centuries, the next generation of the heroes started evolving but with time they had to live in cities and did not feel the use of the magic so they abandoned it later.

Read more to know what happens next...

## Chapter 1: A Boring Life

Just like any normal day, Amaira woke up at 6 in the morning to get ready. She was the most unusual girl at school. She was a 12-year-old girl stuck in ninth grade due to her smartness. Her life was as boring as possible, but sometimes things used to get out of control. Sometimes when she would think of having ice-cream, someone would just come and give it to her. For no reason, when she thought of a latest item or thing she observed that somewhere she would get it, etc. which seemed kind of confusing to her, but she would just leave it thinking it was a coincidence. Her parents were proud of her because she had an IQ level of 190. She was popular as she had started working as an intern in a big finance company with her parents' allowance. The Indian President too had credited her for her smartness.

In America, it was 7 pm where Frank was getting bored and could not watch tv as he was grounded for beating up a person at school. The other boy was trying to be his friend which he hated. Frank never had friends, nor he liked making any. Frank could see and talk to ghosts and spirits which his mom thought was abnormal. She took him to see a doctor and was diagnosed with Clairvoyance. Whenever a strong emotion ran through his veins, he could see things in front of him flying be it even an atom of dust.

One day, Frank was just walking to his therapy sessions which included interaction with people which annoys, and they were boring as watching paint dry. The sessions used to make him uncomfortable and tried to always pull him out of the comfort zone. Since his mom wanted him to recover, he had to go but sometimes he would bunk them.

It was a rainy day in Sydney, Ted felt like locked up in a cage by sitting an entire day in house by not even going to school cause of a holiday. He was a nerdy boy at school with achievements in every single competition. Ted always made his parents proud. He was a perfect child anyone would want. Always winning competitions, had become a daily routine for him and now was starting to get bored but the jingling of medals in his neck made him happy. Winning was like Ted's hobby now. Whenever Ted got too proud, he would fly but he thought that he might be dreaming or imagining which was quite weird because this flying thing happened every day.

Cleopatra was already bored from the time she woke up as her plans with her friends got cancelled. It was burning hot in Egypt. She wished if it could snow and it snowed, which was odd as it happened a third time in the week.

Cleopatra was starting to investigate about this because when someone else wished for the same thing it would never happen not even rarely. She sensed that something was weird which her mom nor dad could understand. She could even grow trees in the desert which seemed abnormal to her.

## Chapter 2: Return of Queen of Darkness

Agrona was a citizen of the planet Corot 7b. She was the princess of the kingdom but her parents along with the citizens of the planet always favoured her elder sister Ava over her which made her angry. The anger and jealousy got the best of her, and she fled to the planet Pluto. There she summoned the dark magic and spirits to accept her and give her the power to destroy and capture Earth, as her family had a good relationship with the superheroes. She got powerful and could destroy anything. She called herself the Queen of Darkness.

After becoming the most powerful being, she marched towards Earth with her army of dead. Agrona destroyed and massacred many people on Earth but to her fate she lost the battle against the Quadruplets Squadron.

Millions of years later after recovering from the depression and wounds of the lost battle, Agrona sat in the Plutonian mountains, summoning her ancestors to give her strength to destroy and capture Earth. This time she swore to take revenge which would be successful as the generations had forgotten about the powers. She cackled on this thought and said, "Let's take our revenge, win and rule over the world." With this she started her journey to Earth. The ozone layer is what annoyed her the most, it did not allow any citizens from different planet or aliens to enter Earth. Agrona used her black magic and opened a portal in space which allowed easy entry to Earth. She entered the southern part where human habitation was less and it was cold just like she loved. Hot climate and deserts were disliked by Agrona. She controlled a few animals' heads which she could find and commanded them and her army,
"Find and bring the Quadruplets Squadron to me."

## Chapter 3: The Rise of Quadruplets Squadron

Amaira had a sudden wake along with Frank, Ted, and Cleopatra in their respective countries. Amaira had a magical ball gifted to her by her aunt. She saw three children in the ball woken up along with her. Since her aunt had told her about magic, Amaira thought that her coincidences were a part of magic, so she thought of calling all those children and they appeared in her bedroom. Cleopatra screamed for help, but Amaira calmed her, saying, "Do not worry Cleopatra, Ted, and Frank. I am harmless. I am just like one of you who does not understand her life and the incidents that occur." This speech looked like it convinced everyone. All of them were able to relate.

Frank loosened up and said, "Can we all be friends?" for the first time in his life. Each one introduced themselves and Amaira was searching for a place where she could hide all her newly made friends. Hearing all the noise Amaira's parents came to check on her and shouted with shocked feeling, "Who are these kids? Where are these from?" this startled the kids. Amaira in just a flick made them all invisible and erased her parent's memory. They could have been told but always explaining things to parents was tiring. When her parents left, the four of them sensed a voice talking in their heads. The voice said, "Come to Egypt. You all will be safe here as your headquarters are over here." Now, Cleopatra was very confused. Amaira tried communicating with the voice but had no luck while a million of questions were popping in Cleopatra's head. Somehow without Amaira thinking they were brought to a dark place and the same voice said, "Welcome Mystical Dreams, The Spirits Guy, Medal Man, and Miss Perfect Biosphere." They looked at each other in a confused manner.

They saw a figure walking towards them; to their surprise, it was a talking dog. The dog introduced itself as part of their team and its name was Namorita.

Namorita claimed that she has been waiting for them to arise again and this time kill Agrona. She explained to them about all the weird incidents, told them about their ancestors, and started their training so they could face their enemy.

Since Agrona had evolved so did they need to? The dog told them that a few animals were tracking them down, so they had to be cautious.

# Chapter 4: The Search

The animals: penguins, wandering albatrosses and few dolphins and whales which were controlled by Agrona had travelled to Saudi Arabia which Namorita tracked and told the quadruplets. She said, "These animals' intentions are not good, though I am not sure if they are after you." The Quadruplets trained harder and harder while the animals were getting closer in tracking them down. Around the headquarters was a protective layer that made things invisible and since it was in a desert area of Egypt it was hard for any of Agrona's magic to enter. The kids now were officially The Quadruplets Squadron.

Amaira was Mystical Dreams with powers of dream catching & giving along with the ability to make her thoughts turn into reality, she could also fly. Her tools were a magic wand and a crystal ball. Frank was The Spirits Guy whose powers were that he could communicate with the spirits (bad & good) and could make things fly but he himself could not fly. His tools are the big spirit who is a new best friend who reacts to every emotion incurred by Frank, respectively.
Ted was Medal Man whose powers were supersonic sound hearing ability, the power to be perfect at everything, can fly. His tools were robots. Cleopatra was Miss Perfect Biosphere who could talk to all forms of nature and the lives of the Earth; she was called the daughter of Nature God. Ted kept boasting, "I am perfect, oh yeah oh yeah." which annoyed everybody. The wandering albatrosses had reached Cairo. Wherever the animals went they kept spreading the freezing weather: snow, ice, and frost along with hail and the south-freezing wind. "My plan is working. At last, the victory is mine." saying this Agrona dived into the sea to search for a gem which would make her stronger.

## Chapter 5: The Gem Hunt

Into the chilliest waters, Agrona dived for the most powerful gem. The gem was red just like Agrona's eyes which showed anger, authoritative power and desire to win and rule the whole galaxy.

The team of superheroes still had disputes among themselves in spite of Namorita explaining them repeatedly, but it was a failure.

The animals were near the headquarters but could not see them as it was invisible. The penguins were gifted with strong smell sense ability which indicated them towards the dry deserts which turned into snowy land due to black magic.

The headquarters were in Aswan the driest land in Egypt which turned into a very cold place on just a foot that landed there.

## Chapter 6: The History Repeats

Agrona found her gem and got the whereabouts of the headquarters from her detectives (animals) and headed there. The gem's powers were extracted and made into a juice that she drank. The disputes got worse between the quadruplets about their powers.

Agrona took the advantage of this situation and led her army toward the headquarters. The protective layer around it was of no use now as it was destroyed. She said in an angry manner, "Go and bring those weaklings to me. I will destroy them and use their powers to get strong."

Amaira saw outside the window that an army of dead bodies, skeletons, and zombies was coming to attack them. She tried to warn the rest of the group who paid no attention to it as Cleopatra and Ted were still quarreling whereas Frank sat in a corner feeling low. It was of no avail to explain things and situations to these people.

Amaira asked Namorita, "Can I fight alone?" "No. You all need to use all your powers together to win against that witch." came the answer.
She invited Frank to join but he refused. She went alone outside despite Namorita' s warnings to save the world but she kept doubting herself as she was only good at studies. Agrona saw her and said, "You are Mystical Dreams. Where are the others?" She answered, "Others are here but you need to go through me first to kill them."

Amaira tried to control the half-eaten or present brains of the dead army, but she could not. With the power of her thoughts, she tried the kill the army but they were already dead so she could not. Frank saw all this from the window, and he too went to help her. They both tried to keep the powers from destroying the headquarters.

Finally, Namorita got tired and shouted loudly, "Both of you, can you not see the war going on where your friends are dying and here you are fighting about whose power is better? Every superhero is unique along with their powers. In this team, everyone must work together to complete all the obstacles and missions." This was like a moral to both. Cleopatra along with Ted went down to the battlefield and saw their friends wounded. Cleopatra grew trees and called the sun, and the place became like a scenery which was Agrona's weakness. Her powers were getting deteriorated due to the sun. "We need to combine our powers: thoughts, spirits, medals, and heat is what we need to defeat her," said Amaira getting irritated. They combined their powers and threw them at Agrona and this time she was killed.

There was a modest problem that the news of Agrona's death had reached her family and to take revenge they were coming. To know more about it, read more.....

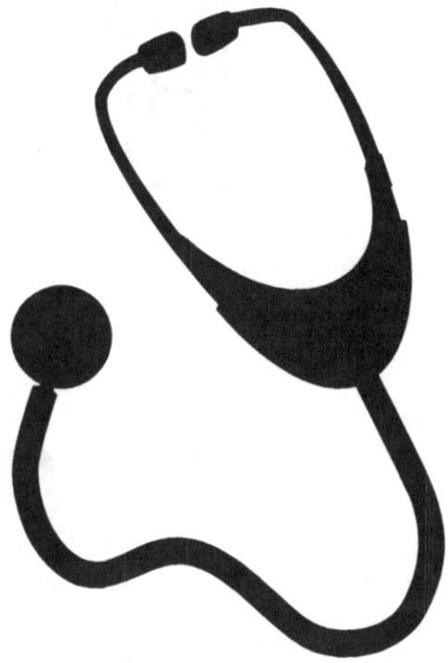

# One Small Action

By

Shiza Fatima

There is this city of Lagos, with its huge buildings and dazzling lifestyle and just 200km from the city of Lagos, lies a village with abundance of poverty and small houses. In the midst of the huts, lies a clinic named 'Wellness Clinic'. Dr. Vivek is the owner of the clinic and the only doctor that works there with medical facility. A large part of his childhood was spent battling hunger, poverty and sometimes homelessness. He spent days hungry, scared and not knowing where his next meal would come from. On some days, his family and he got two meals for the day from workers at the rescue mission and on some days, he would get food from people passing by.

Being a single child of the family was tough for Vivek. He had to help his father sell newspapers since he was 12. They used to get very little money. Vivek's life changed when he was 16. His father became ill due to a fungal infection. There was no doctor in their village or in the nearby villages. The doctors in the cities were very expensive and they could not afford the treatment. All this search, along with no treatment led to his father's demise. This left Vivek devastated and heartbroken.

Being the only male member in his family, he had to provide for his mother as well. One day, he was sitting on the footpath, feeling sad about his father's death when a man who was passing by, came to him and offered him some money. He saw the sadness on Vivek's face and asked him about it. Upon hearing his story, the man said, "I know the pain of losing a loved one, and it was unfortunate that your father wasn't able to get treated. But believe me there is a future for you and a future where you would also grow up and have the luxuries in life. If you work hard no one can break your chain of being happy. If you want the change, then you should be the change." Vivek had tears in his eyes. It was at this point that he decided to become a doctor so that no other person would face the lack of access to medical treatment.

The man's words motivated him to work hard and earn some money for his family. He began making things from waste lying around the street. He would make bags out of torn clothes lying around. Sometimes, he would make jewellery and toys. Imagination had no limits. His products garnered a lot of attention and he inspired people. They saw how Vivek was reusing waste and saving the environment.

He continued his art and eventually it caught the attention of a famous environmentalist who worked for the Government. He agreed to sponsor Vivek's education and gave him and his mother a new home. He received the recognition he deserved for his contribution to the environment. Vivek began going to school and worked very hard.
He not only survived, but learned to thrive. There were many obstacles along his way but at the end, his consistent hard work helped him to find success. Many years later, he accomplished his childhood dream of being a doctor. He opened a clinic in his home village, and now treats the poor free of charge. Word spread about his skill and reputation and people from far off came for their treatment to him.
He helped many people who struggled like his family

One day Vivek got a visitor who was an old man who seemed strangely familiar. He was diagnosed with a terminal illness. The man said "I have been to different doctors but they all tell me I am going to die really soon. I heard a lot about you, so I wanted to visit one last doctor." Vivek said, "I think we have met before sir. Have you been here before?" "Yes, I have been to this village, but a long time ago", the man replied. Vivek said, "Please lie down while I do your check-up." Vivek continued examining him and said, "I think you might remember me. I was a young boy, sitting on the footpath, sad about my father's death", said Vivek, as he gathered his instruments. "when you came along as an angle.

You spoke to me, and motivated me to be the change I wanted. My life has changed after that day." The man did not answer. Vivek turned around as he heard no response. The man's eyes were closed. He had died in Vivek's clinic.

Little did he know that he was at the very clinic of the sad poor boy whose life was changed by his words.

Vivek did not get the chance to thank him. Life had come to a complete circle. One does not know which small action can change a person's life.

The world is filled with different kinds of people, some fortunate and some less fortunate. But we all have one thing in common- humanity, and that's what binds all of us together.

---

## The End

RIDHZWORLD
PUBLISHING

www.ridhzworld.com

## RidhzWorld Collection